The
Secret

Sean Lewis
Illustrated by Mel Todd

CAMBRIDGE
UNIVERSITY PRESS

When I was little, the mobile library used to visit our school.

"The library is coming! The library is coming!" shouted Trevor, my older brother.

All the children wanted to see it and go inside.

I climbed up the metal steps and went inside.
There were books all around. I did not know
what to do.

A friendly woman, Mrs Jacobs, asked me to write my name and address on a yellow piece of paper. She then gave me two green library cards.

I chose two books. I could not wait to get home to start reading.

I didn't know that I had to give my cards to
Mrs Jacobs.

I just walked out of the truck with my two
new books.

We were walking home when Trevor asked, "Sean, why do you still have your cards? You silly, you're supposed to hand in your cards when you borrow a book!"

All the other children laughed. I felt so
ashamed. I didn't want anybody else to find out
that I didn't know what to do in a library.

I went outside, dug a hole in the garden and buried my cards.

Two days later, Daddy was digging in the
garden and he found the cards.

"Sean," he said, "why are your library cards in the garden?"

I told him what I had done and he just laughed. When he stopped laughing he told me to take the books back to the library.

I went back to the library the next day. I told
Mrs Jacobs my story and she said, "Don't
worry, Sean. We all make mistakes."

She helped me to find two new books and
I handed in my cards.

After that, I went to the library every two
weeks. I read so many books – about children
like me and animals and many things.